POPPY VALLEY

The Magic of the
ENCHANTED IRON MINES

Annabelle Emma Jones

POPPY VALLEY
The Magic of the
ENCHANTED IRON MINES

First published in Great Britain as a softback original in 2022

Typeset in Caroni

Design, typesetting and publishing by UK Book Publishing

www.ukbookpublishing.com

ISBN: 978-1-915338-01-3

MEET THE CHARACTERS

Tracy
Likes: Sleep, Jasmine, Poppy Valley, gnomes
Dislikes: Being awake, sadness, not succeeding

Jasmine
Likes: Cookies, Tracy, Poppy Valley, being awake
Dislikes: Sleep, sadness, Winter

Clara
Likes: Poppies, cute things, happy people
Dislikes: Cornflowers, people being sad

Spike
Likes: Having a plan, not being in charge
Dislikes: Not having a plan, being in charge

Dave
Likes: Happy gnomes, poppies, being in charge, being correct
Dislikes: Madhiouse, gnomes being sad, problems, being
wrong

Jasmine

Tracy

Clara

Dave

Spike

CHAPTER 1

The Gnome Gathering

"Are you awake?" murmured Jasmine Elliot to her best friend Tracy Hall.

"Yeah," yawned Tracy, sitting up in bed and rubbing her deep brown eyes.

"Do you still have your watch on your bedside table?" asked Jasmine, sitting up in bed.

"No, but I do have a bedside clock and that says 2:30 in the morning, so I suggest we try to go back to sleep," replied Tracy, snuggling back down and shutting her eyes.

"But I can't sleep!" whispered Jasmine. "I know! We could get cookies and milk and sit downstairs on the sofa and eat them!" she suggested, looking hopeful.

"Alright, alright, you win, Jasmine! Let us change into our dressing gowns and head down. Cookies are in the bottom left cupboard." Tracy Laughed, jumping out of bed and tiptoeing over to her peg where her pink dressing gown hung. The two friends headed downstairs and helped themselves to cookies and milk.

"Yummy yummy!" exclaimed Jasmine taking a big bite of her cookie before gulping down some milk.

"Shall we watch some telly?" suggested Tracy, tenderly nibbling the edge of her cookie.

"Yeah I suppose," shrugged Jasmine, looking out of the window. "What's that?" she said, pointing to the poppy bush at the bottom of the garden.

"Erm a poppy bush?" stated Tracy, looking up from her milk.

"No silly! I know that but one of the poppies is glowing," murmured Jasmine, opening the back door and tiptoeing outside. "Brrr!" she exclaimed. "It's absolutely freezing out here!"

Tracy reluctantly followed her out and hand in hand they went over to the poppy bush and touched the glowing poppy with trembling fingers.

All of a sudden, they felt themselves being dragged into the poppy. They gripped hands and pulled each other close.

A few seconds later, the poppy spat them out and they landed in a soft flower bed full of tulips and peonies that came up to their knees when they stood up. The two friends brushed themselves off and walked shakily towards a set of wooden doors that stood in the corner.

"One two three push!" wheezed Jasmine, heaving on one side of the wooden doors and pushing it open. A crowd of poppy seeds rushed out, revealing a room with golden flooring that shone in the moonlight. Best of all, lots of cute little gnome-like things with cute faces were standing in the doorway welcoming them!

"Wow!" breathed Tracy. "I must be dreaming," she declared, pinching herself hard on the cheek. "Ouch!" she exclaimed. "Definitely not dreaming!"

"Hello girls, my name is Clara and we are Poppy Gnomes. Our jobs are to make sure that all of the plants in Poppy Valley are growing properly," spoke an extra pretty girl gnome with long blonde hair that fell down to her bum.

"Poppy Valley," Jasmine murmured under her breath again and again.

"Let me explain why you are here," said a rather plump gnome with a badge that had HEAD GNOME written on it in capital letters. "The leader of Cornflower Valley is planning to take over our valley!" he sighed, with anger rising in his voice.

"And you want us to..." wondered Tracy, hanging onto Jasmine's arm, still clutching her cookie to her chest, breathing in its sweet scent.

"Help us save the valley! Duh!" grumbled the head gnome.

Clara caught sight of their puzzled expressions.

"What head gnome Dave means to say is it would be lovely if you could help defeat Cornflower Valley, please!" she added, smiling and showing a set of brilliant white teeth that shone reflecting moonlight onto the floor.

"Ahh we see!" chorused Jasmine and Tracy together. "Well we need a plan and to make a plan we need to predict their next move which will be..."said Jasmine, suddenly becoming very serious.

"The flower gardens! They will probably attack the flower gardens first!" exclaimed Clara.

"Right, so we go to the flower gardens and get some tools to protect the flowers – anyone got any ideas? If so, then please raise your hand," called Tracy to the whole room. A boy gnome with short, smooth brown hair raised his hand.

"Yes?" demanded Jasmine, standing on the stool in the corner to get a better view of the crowd of gnomes.

"Well, there is a gnome who lives in the deep dark woods who sells all sorts of potions that we could pour on the flowers to strengthen them and protect them perhaps?" he suggested.

"What is your name?" requested Jasmine purely out of curiosity.

"Spike," replied Spike. "It is a silly name!" he said, drooping all of a sudden.

"Well I think Spike is a lovely name." Tracy smiled, offering her arms for the little gnome to sit in. He was surprisingly heavy, but Tracy lifted him up and kissed him on the cheek. He blushed and smiled in an embarrassed but pleased fashion.

"Ahem!" coughed Dave to get their attention. "The girls, Clara and Spike if he wants to come along, will set off whilst we head to the flower gardens and make a forcefield for the flowers, okay?"

"Yes, sir," Tracy, Jasmine, Clara and Spike saluted and waved goodbye before setting off to the deep dark wood.

"This way." Clara smiled, beckoning to where the girls came in, and wandering outside.

"If I remember rightly then the woods are really far east so we should head east I think," declared Spike triumphantly. The group marched out of the gardens and headed east.

"Is it going to be cold?" pondered Jasmine.

"This is Poppy valley!" laughed Clara. She waved her hands around and all of a sudden they had fleece lining under their nightwear!

"You can do magic!" gasped Tracy, staring wide eyed at Clara's hands with astonishment.

"Yeah. No biggy!" chuckled Clara, looking smug at Tracy's astonishment.

"No biggy!" repeated Tracy, clearly shocked at Clara's humbleness.

The unlikely looking group continued along the path, aware that Cornflower Valley citizens could be anywhere in the trees surrounding the track.

"Nearly there," puffed Spike, looking at a little hut in the corner of the woods.

"That's it!" exclaimed Clara so they headed toward the hut and knocked on the door.

CHAPTER 2
Grovel

"Hello." A warty gnome-like creature with a long grey beard opened the door and looked at the girls. "Ahh, Spike, how lovely of you to drop by, and are these friends of yours?" he said with his gaze landing on the little gnome.

"Yes they are!" replied Spike, smiling reassuringly at the girls and Clara who were shrinking back in fright at the gnome's appearance.

"The name's Grovel!" chuckled Grovel, offering a hand for the girls and Clara to shake.

"This is Tracy, that's Clara and the other one's Jasmine," explained Spike, pointing to each one of them in turn.

"Do come in and explain why you are here on this cold winter's night," said Grovel, beckoning them inside where there was a warm, cosy fire.

"Thank you," began Clara. "We are here because these are the human children that have been selected to save Poppy Valley from Cornflower Valley. We wondered whether you had any potions we could perhaps pour on the flowers to protect them from the enemy," babbled Clara, looking pleased with her explanation.

"Okay, I will see what I can rustle up." Grovel smiled, heading through to another room that joined onto the room that they were currently sat in. "Come along," added Grovel nodding at the four friends. They followed him into the room. Grovel walked towards a cauldron in the corner of the room and threw in a few different powders and liquids.

"What sort of potion is it?" wondered Jasmine as she stared at the shelves of ingredients and gasped at the mixture that Grovel was stirring. "Wow!" she exclaimed, in awe of the way it spat and bubbled.

"A strength potion. It should stop them from damaging the flowers too badly," he muttered, timing how long he had been stirring it for.

"How long will it take? Because we don't have long," asked Clara anxiously, her dainty features creasing with worry.

"Another 10 minutes, I think," grumbled Grovel.

Clara started pacing up and down the room with worry.
Jasmine scooped up the little gnome and gave her a hug.

"Don't worry, I trust Grovel," she whispered.

"Okay, then so do I!" agreed Clara, grinning once again.

"It's ready!" called Grovel.

"Coming!" shouted Jasmine and they went through and retrieved the potion.

"Thank you, friend!" shouted Spike as they were walking out of the door.

Grovel grunted and shut the door behind him.

"Wow! I cannot believe we have the potion!" screeched Clara, dancing a jig.

"Shh!" said Spike holding a finger to his lips.

Clara mouthed the words "oopsy!" back to him and quietly continued along the dark path. Rustles in the trees ahead frightened Tracy, making her shiver as she pressed her body against Jasmine who reached out a hand to hold.

"So where are we going now?" asked Jasmine, still holding Tracy's hand.

"We will head to the iron mines and ask a nice-looking miner for some swords and armour to fight the Cornflower Valley soldiers," announced Clara.

"I think the iron mines are this way!" called Spike, pointing towards a little turn off further down the path.

"Okay, then let's head this way," shrugged Tracy, heading onto the off road and kneeling down to check the ground for any evidence of cornflower valley people. Suddenly, there was a flurry of blue petals and a voice laughed mischievously then they were gone.

"Cornflower!" growled Clara, hissing at the petals on the ground.

They continued along the faint, overgrown path, this time much more carefully.

"Are we nearly there yet?" groaned Tracy, yawning sleepily.

"Nowhere near!" called Spike who was walking ahead speaking to passing creatures.

"Mr Popular!" laughed Clara, raising her eyebrows at him.

He laughed gingerly and blushed bright red. They walked for what felt like hours and then eventually arrived at some caves full of little walking pickaxes that banged their heads against the ores to collect iron.

"Doesn't it hurt them?" asked Jasmine anxiously.

"Oh no! no! No," chuckled Clara, smiling at a baby pickaxe that was being bottle fed by its mother. "Of course not."

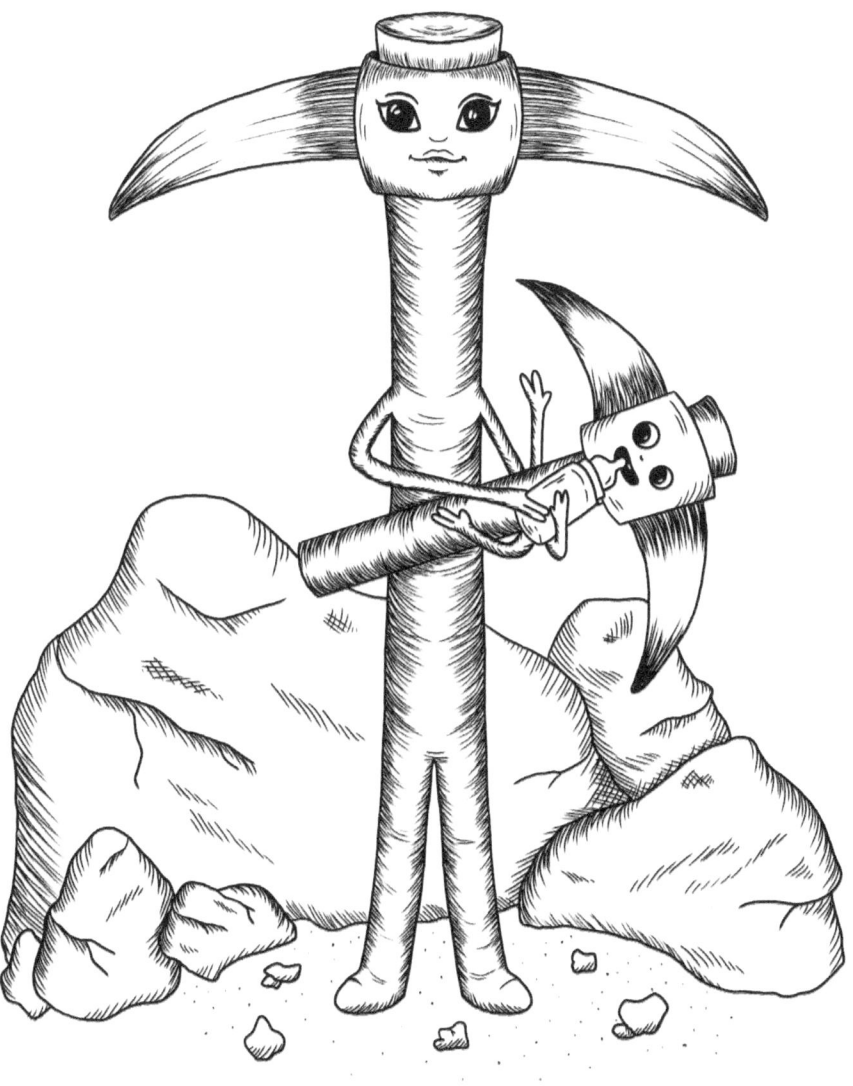

"Which way do we go?" pondered Spike.

"Trial and error," stated Clara, heading along the main path whilst searching for a nice looking pickaxe to ask for the sword and armour.

"This is hopeless!" moaned Jasmine after 10 minutes of mooching about.

"Nothing is hopeless!" corrected Spike, although there was a flicker of doubt in his voice.

They walked along the path, still keeping an eye out for friendly looking creatures.

"He looks nice," muttered Tracy.

"Let's go for it then!" said Clara, striding towards the boy pickaxe. "Hello! We need some armour and a sword so we wondered whether you could help us?" asked Clara in an extra cheesy voice.

To the girl's relief he replied saying, "Happy to help! One for each of you then?"

"Thank you and yes we need one for each of us." Jasmine grinned.

"Right, just give me a minute to get the iron and then I have to give it to the iron spirits which only my species can see and they will turn 'em into the stuff you need," explained the pickaxe.

"Great, we will come back soon!"

"Righty oh!" called the pickaxe as he tap tap tapped away at the iron, the friends headed along the paths exploring all the nooks and crannies of the mine.

"Wow," declared Tracy after a while. "This place is spectacular!"

They carried on talking to each pickaxe in turn and asking them to be on watch in case any cornflowers came to invade them. After a while, they headed back toward where they saw the pickaxe that was helping them.

"Have you managed?" blurted Spike, clearly anxious of time.

"Yes, I have, and call me Bluey — that is my name!" he replied, smiling and holding out two small sets of armour and two human sized sets. He then pulled four swords out of his pocket and handed them over.

"Is there anything that we could do in return?" asked Tracy, blushing at how silly she felt asking something like that.

"No, this is my job!" laughed Bluey, smiling at the girls and their gnome friends as they walked away from the mine.

"What shall we do next?" asked Jasmine as they left.

"Ok, so we have some potions, some armour and a sword, so I think we should spy on the people from Cornflower Valley!" decided Spike, heading down the off road and emerging onto the main path once again.

"What good will spying do?" moaned Clara, dragging her little limbs and yawning heavily.

"Is there any place nearby we could go to stay for the night?" asked Jasmine, hinting at Clara's tiredness.

"No, but nothing is stopping you from conjuring somewhere up," yawned Clara, clearly hinting that she was too tired to do any magic.

"Of course, my lady." Spike bowed, waving his hands around in the air. A cabin appeared in the trees with a cosy-looking wooden front door and sage green windows. They headed in and each flopped down on a bed. They said goodnight to each other before drifting off into a deep slumber.

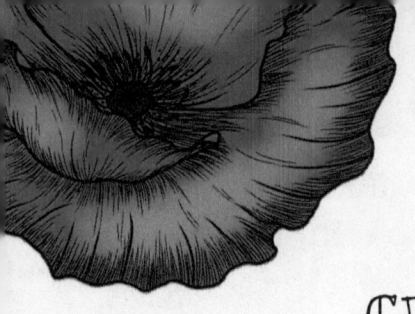

CHAPTER 3

Spying!

When they awoke the sun was rising and the air was fresh and smelt of flowers. They got out of bed and rushed out of the cabin at 150 mph.

"Morning!" called Jasmine as she wandered out of her and Tracy's side of the cabin and followed Tracy and the others out of the door.

"OK, so are we still spying on Cornflower Valley?" asked Clara, skipping through the leaves and giggling at the hares that ran alongside the path. "This way!" she called from ahead.

"Coming!" called Tracy, running to catch up with Clara.

They eventually reached a large dome with NO ENTRY CORNFLOWER VALLEY CITIZENS ONLY written on the entrance in capital letters.

"Oh dear, it seems to be locked," said Spike, pulling hard on the handle.

Tracy tried, but she could not do much either.

"Hmm," pondered Clara, stroking her chin thoughtfully. "I could try to magic us in? Or is that too risky?"

"Erm, I am willing to try," said Jasmine, raising both hands in an I-don't-know way.

"Same," shrugged Tracy, walking towards Clara.

"I think I will magic myself, thank you very much," babbled Spike, preparing himself in the corner.

"OK, see you in there," murmured Clara, beginning to wave her hands.

"This is it!" whispered Jasmine as a gust of wind picked them up and the world spun around them.

The next minute, they were stood in the corner of the dome staring at a crowd of cornflowers with wicked-looking faces. The flowers were looking at a flipchart that had tonight's plan written at the top in swirly writing. It showed a sketch labelled iron mines. Jasmine let out a small gasp —

they had been wrong all along; they were planning to invade the iron mines first! They magicked themselves out and rushed to Spike who was still preparing himself to travel.

"Spike! The cornflowers are going to go to the iron mines tonight, not the flower gardens!" blurted Jasmine, still shocked herself.

"What? Never!" exclaimed Spike upon hearing her words.

So, on that note the friends moved on and headed to the flower gardens to tell the other gnomes about the change of plan. They trudged through the woods and out into the kingdom itself, which was full of poppy field after poppy field.

"Wow! This is very beautiful!" admired Tracy, going to pick a poppy from the fields

"No! Stop!" called a voice.

Tracy looked up and saw a watering can with a poppy face was talking to her.

"Sorry!" she responded, swallowing hard.

"Never mind!" laughed Clara cheerfully. Jasmine smiled at Clara in awe of how she could change the mood so amazingly.

"So, let's make a plan! We should go straight to Dave and tell him about what we have found. Then we must try to make it to the iron mines before the attack with our potions and weapons. Does that sound like a plan?" declared Spike, nodding wisely.

"Good plan," decided Clara, striding ahead and letting herself into a garden full of gnomes making nets and protection for flowers, all being shouted at by Dave who was red in the face from sweat. "Dave! Dave!" shouted Clara, waving at him.

"Girls, have you managed?" asked Dave anxiously.

"Look, we have the stuff, but when we decided to spy on them we saw them looking at a plan for tonight and it was a clipart of the iron mines!" babbled Jasmine.

Dave let out a gasp and called the gnomes to attention to tell them the news. They all gasped and a few whimpered in fear when they heard.

"Hush now, the girls, Clara and Spike have a plan," he announced, looking at them as if to say you have a plan, don't you?

"So first," began Clara, remembering Spike's recount of his plan. "We alert you guys, which we have done, and then we all head to the iron mines and set up protection!" she finished triumphantly.

"OK, good plan, that is what we will do," declared Dave, to the crowd of gnomes.

Almost immediately the gnomes got to work, busying themselves with making iron barriers and carving chicken wire into domes to put over the iron ores for protection. Jasmine began sculpting a large dome made out of clay for baby pickaxes to hide in. Once or twice she ended up throwing it away to start again, but eventually she got into the swing of it. Meanwhile, Clara, Dave, Spike and some other gnomes drew a sketch of the iron mines and decided who would cover what areas. Tracy watched over the events and helped out a group of children gnomes who were attempting to mould some chicken wire into a dragon shape.

They continued like this for an hour or so and then decided to set off to the iron mines and put their creations to the test. The huge crowd of gnomes walked together all the way to the mines without stopping even once to catch their breath. When they arrived, the pickaxes were all asleep and snoring loudly.

"Well, we are going to have to wake them up!" whispered Tracy, kissing a baby one on the cheek and then heading over to Bluey and doing the same. Soon all of the gnomes had joined in, and in no time at all each and every pickaxe was awake and informed of the plan to attack and how they had to send all of the babies into the dome. After a few minutes, the Cornflower Valley people began to arrive.

CHAPTER 4

Cornflower just got scary ...

Everyone made a line in front of the entrance and waved their swords around in the air threateningly, but despite their best efforts the Cornflower Valley soldiers did not seem to have any intentions of backing off them, so the girls stepped forward and grabbed the closest warriors by the scruff of the neck and threw them into the river.

The gnomes continued to fight the flowing crowds of blue flowers until they backed off and made a huddle to whisper to each other.

The girls and the gnomes waited anxiously and twitched their ears forward in an attempt to hear snippets of conversation. Eventually the soldiers in the huddle came forward and clashed their swords against their shields, which in ancient war would mean "Come and get me!" so Poppy Valley's army stepped forward, threatening their swords.

"STOP!" demanded Jasmine, stepping forward. "Lower your swords." Everybody stopped and looked at her, clearly confused. "We don't want war, we want peace and friendship," she explained, her gaze landing on the leader of Cornflower Valley.

"I agree with her!" shouted Clara, stepping forward and clinging to Jasmine's leg.

The leader of Cornflower Valley was angered and made the decision to step forward and threaten his sword.

Tracy took a deep breath and walked towards him. "This is childish!" she shouted, shaking her head. "There is no reason for this to happen."

"Ha! But I need power, I need a new valley!" cackled Madhiouse, the leader of Cornflower Valley, and with that he pulled out his sword and swung it at Clara, stabbing her tummy with its blade. She gasped and fell to the ground.

"What have you done?" said Tracy, anger rising in her voice.

"She won't die, but she will definitely be hurt." Madhiouse grinned, smirking meanly.

Dave shook his head, in shame, and ran over to Clara who was lying on the ground unconscious. Tears pricked Jasmine's eyes thinking about the lively little gnome she had met a few days ago. She reached out a fist and threatened it, ready to punch, but before she could act, he and his whole valley were gone. They had just disappeared.

Suddenly, a note fell on her feet, making her jump. She picked it up and Tracy huddled closer, eager to see.

"We will be back, Hate from Madhiouse."

"I think you should go home, girls," murmured Spike. "There is nothing left to be done but I will summon you when there is."

"How will we know you are summoning us?" she asked, concerned.

"This," said Dave, handing each of them a poppy. "It will glow when Spike, Clara or myself summon you."

"Thank you!" called Jasmine as she and Tracy were whisked away in a tornado of petals.

The chatter from below became a distant murmur and within seconds they were back in Tracy's garden as if nothing had ever happened.

"Wow!" they giggled, walking back inside, dazzled by the pure excitement of it all.

"Between you and me," confirmed Jasmine.

"Between you and me," promised Tracy, and they walked back inside the house, hand in hand. They were already thinking about their next adventure.

The End

A note from the author

Annabelle's message: This is my first ever book and it is such a special thing to me that I am lucky enough to have this amazing privilege. I am nine years old and books have always been a huge part of my life and every second of every day I dream of this. I hope this book brings you the same joy it brings me. I would love to thank everyone, but I especially want to thank my best friends Emily and Lilly-sue. They have supported me through this and are always there for me when I need them the most. Also I would like to thank Dougie my dog for comforting me when I am sad.

Many thanks, Annabelle xx

"If you want to hear more from Tracy and Jasmine, then you'll be over the moon to know that more adventures are coming soon!"

www.ingramcontent.com/pod-product-compliance
Lightning Source LLC
Chambersburg PA
CBHW020609130626
46552CB00007B/3123